Sharon and Darren

Nigel Gray and Cathy Wilcox

A & C Black · London

Best Friends · Jessy and the Long Short Dress · Jessy Runs Away ·
Rachel Anderson
Changing Charlie · **Scoular Anderson**
Ernest the Heroic Lion-tamer · **Damon Burnard**
Weedy Me · **Sally Christie**
Something Old · **Ruth Craft**
Almost Goodbye Guzzler · Two Hoots · **Helen Cresswell**
Magic Mash · Nina's Machines · **Peter Firmin**
Shadows on the Barn · **Sarah Garland**
Clever Trevor · Nora Bone · **Brough Girling**
Private Eye of New York · Sharon and Darren · **Nigel Gray**
The Thing-in-a-Box · **Diana Hendry**
Desperate for a Dog · Houdini Dog · **Rose Impey**
Georgie and the Dragon · Georgie and the Planet Raider · **Julia Jarman**
Cowardy Cowardy Cutlass · Free With Every Pack ·
Mo and the Mummy Case · The Fizziness Business · **Robin Kingsland**
And Pigs Might Fly! · Albertine, Goose Queen · Jigger's Day Off ·
Martians at Mudpuddle Farm · Mossop's Last Chance · **Michael Morpurgo**
Grubble Trouble · **Hilda Offen**
Hiccup Harry · Harry's Party · Harry Moves House · Harry with Spots On ·
Chris Powling
The Father Christmas Trap · **Margaret Stonborough**
Pesters of the West · **Lisa Taylor**
Jacko · Messages · Rhyming Russell · **Pat Thomson**
Monty, The Dog Who Wears Glasses · Monty Bites Back ·
Monty must be Magic · Monty – Up To His Neck in Trouble · **Colin West**
Stone the Crows, It's a Vacuum-cleaner ·
Ging Gang Goolie - It's An Alien! · **Bob Wilson**

First published 1993 by A & C Black (Publishers) Ltd
35 Bedford Row, London WC1R 4JH

ISBN 0–7136–3537–1

A CIP catalogue record for this book
is available from the British Library.

Filmset by Kalligraphic Design Ltd, Horley, Surrey
Printed in Great Britain by William Clowes Ltd, Beccles and London

I've got a boyfriend.
His name is Darren.
Sharon and Darren –
we make a poem.

Darren's going to buy me a
crunchy bar.

He said to wait by the corner shop
at half past three.

My dad bought me a digital watch for my birthday.

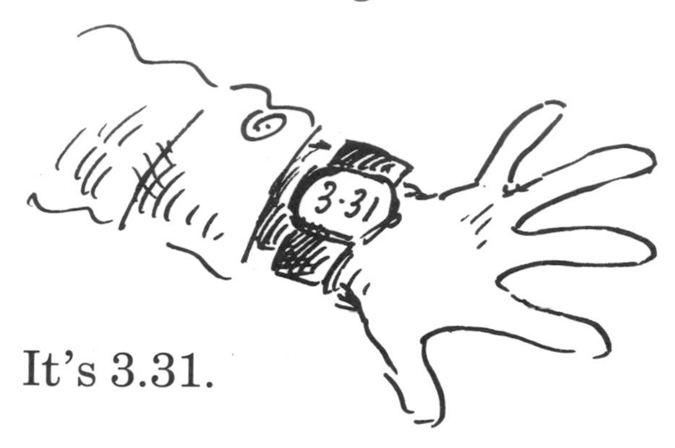

It's 3.31.

Darren hasn't come.

It's 3.32.

Perhaps he's got a new girlfriend.

He's always talking to That Tracy-Marie.

She's not a
nice girl.

She picks
her nose when
no one's
looking

– and flicks it.

It's 3.33.

Perhaps he's been run over.
Perhaps a huge road roller was
coming down the street,

and now poor Darren's as flat as
a pancake all covered with
strawberry jam.

It's 3.34.

FRUIT AND
VEGETABLES

Perhaps, just as he was about to come out of the house, he needed to go to the toilet,

and perhaps he slipped in,
and got stuck,

and had to go to
the hospital with the toilet seat
stuck on his bum.

It's 3.35.

Perhaps he was walking along, thinking about me, thinking about us being a poem – Sharon and Darren, not looking where he was going,

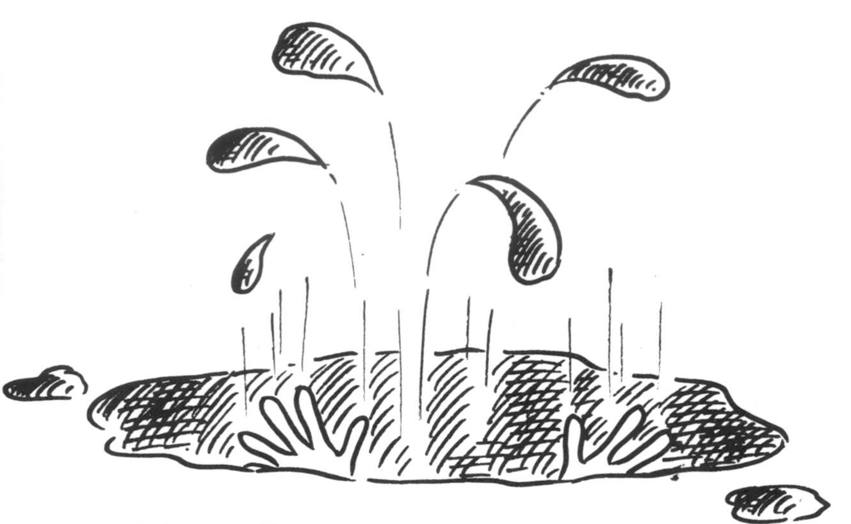

and he fell down a great big hole
in the road, and got washed through
a slimy sewer,

and an alligator was lying in wait
in all that mucky water,

and with one mighty snap of
its great jaws it crunched poor
Darren in two, swallowed the bits,

and spat out Darren's teeth, and toe nails, and his zips.

It’s 3.36.

Perhaps Darren
broke a cup
when he had
a drink

and tried to
mend it with
superglue,

and his hand
got stuck to
the cup,

and the cup got
stuck to the table,
and when he tried
to wipe the
glue off

he got some glue
on his other hand,
and his nose
started itching, and
he scratched it,

and his other
hand got stuck
to his nose,

and he dropped some
glue on the floor,

and one foot
got stuck to
the carpet,

and the dog
came along
to sniff Darren's
smelly feet,

and he tried to
push the dog away
and his other foot got
stuck to the dog,

and now he's waiting
for the fire brigade
to come and
rescue him.

It's 3.37.

Perhaps he came home from school
and thought the goldfishes
looked cold,

and poured boiling water into the
fishbowl to warm them up, and
killed them all,

and his mother might have been angry with him for being such a twit, and made him weed the garden,

and de-flea the dog,

and wash the budgie's hair,

and clean
the inside of
the toilet bowl
with his bare
hands,

and won't let him go out for a week.

It's 3.38.

Perhaps a tiger escaped from a circus and chased him,

and he ran away and hid in a dustbin,

and the dustbin men came along
and tipped him into the back of
their truck,

and he got scrunched up in all the rotten smelly garbage,

and tipped out on to the town rubbish tip.

It's 3.39.

Perhaps he got caught by that old witch who lives at number twenty-three.

Perhaps she hooked her walking stick in the back of his trousers

as he walked past her house on the way to meet me,

and she
put a spell
on him, and
turned him into
a toad,

and gave him to the
cat to play with.

It's 3.40.
MIXED

NESS
ND
LES

Perhaps he was trying to cross the road, and some demonstrators were coming,

and he got caught up and
carried along against his will,

and when the demonstrators were chased by the police, he got bonked on the head, and bundled into a police van, and carted off to prison,

EE-AW-EE-AW-EE-AW-EE.
POLICE

and locked in an overcrowded cell with four fierce villains, and only three beds – and the warder's lost the key.

It's 3.41.

Perhaps he was on his way to meet me and a flying saucer landed in the road, and some weird luminous creatures got out and kidnapped him

and carried him off to their planet in space, and they're going to keep him in a zoo, and all the funny space monsters will pay their pocket money to come to look at him, and laugh.

It’s 3.42.

Perhaps he was watching TV

and something in the television programme reached out of the screen and got hold of him

and dragged him in, so now he's a
prisoner in a TV show and
can't get out,

and if he did get out
he'd be so small,

his mother
wouldn't
see him,

and when she was
cleaning the carpet

she'd hoover him up,

and no one would
ever know where
he went.

It's 3.43.

Perhaps he got lost, and ended up at the airport by mistake,

and some hijackers
came along and took
poor Darren hostage,
and stole an aeroplane,

and after they'd taken off, a hand
grenade rolled under his seat,
and he wondered what the pin was
for, and pulled it out,

and it blew a great big hole in the floor,

and he

fell

through –

and now, he might be

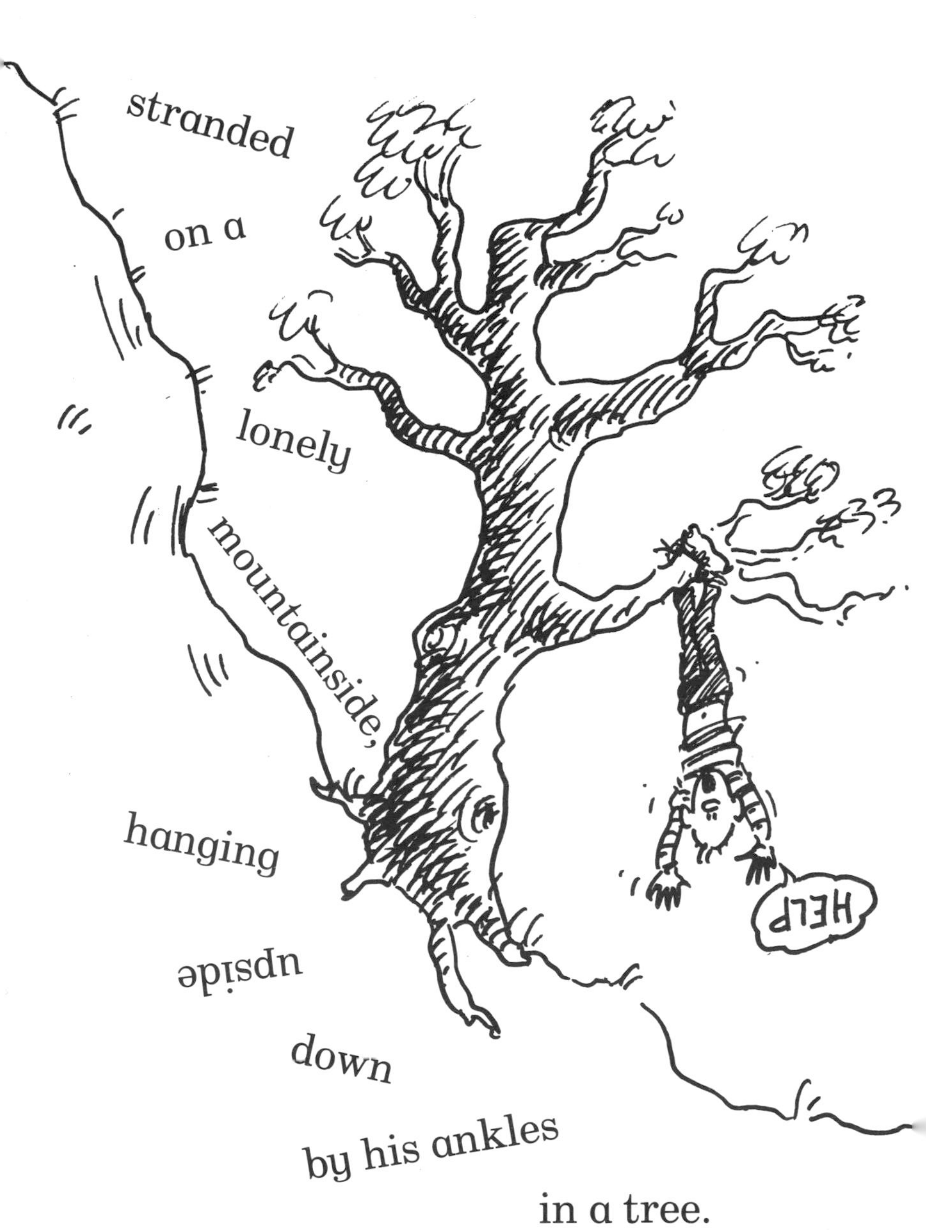

stranded

on a

lonely

mountainside,

hanging

upside

down

by his ankles

in a tree.

It's 3.44.

Perhaps, when he was hurrying along, with his heart pounding in his chest with the anticipation of seeing me,

there was an earthquake, and the

ground opened up beneath his feet,
and he fell into the crevice,

like a filling in a sandwich,

and the earth closed up again

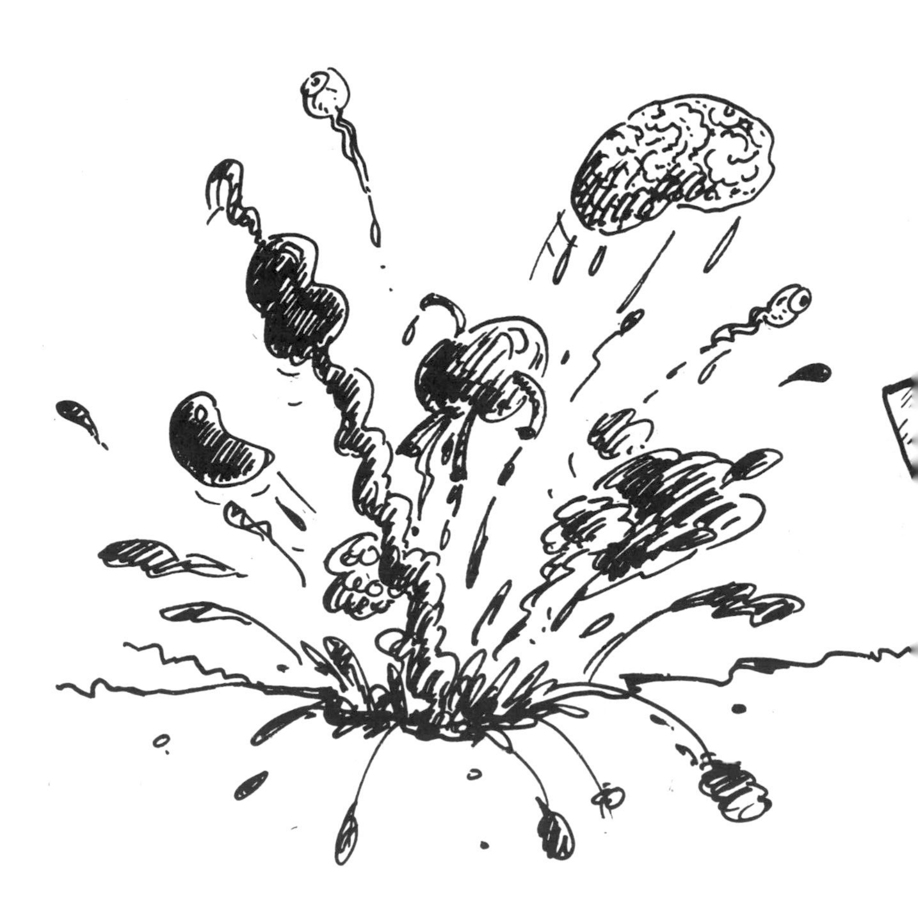

and made him as flat as a piece
of greasy beef in a hamburger,
and all his insides squirted out of
the top of his head like a
rainbow-coloured fountain,

and it will be on the front page of the newspaper, and there'll be a photo of me, because I'm his girlfriend, and our names rhyme.

The Daily Trumpet
BOY SQUASHED IN EARTHQUAKE HORROR!
Heroine waits in vain.
Today, a violent earth tremor tragically swallowed up poor ten-year-old Darren White. His girlfriend the beautiful and celebrated Sharon Green, waited for him at a corner shop in town, never
guessing the horror that had befallen the boy she loved. 'It couldn't have happened to a nicer person,' she said, with tears filling her gorgeous eyes, while photographers from all over the world queued to take her picture, and journalists from every continent clamoured for appointments to
Sharon Green ..."I waited."
the fame and wealth that await her, she will never forget the boy she once loved who sacrificed his life in a gallant endeavour to be at her side during yesterday's

It's 3.45.
I'm going home.

Oh, hello, Darren. I've been waiting for you.
Hello, Sharon. I've been waiting for you, too. I didn't see you There, Sharon.

Where's my crunchy bar, then?
I thought you hadn't come, So I ate it.
He ate my crunchy bar!

Do you still want to be my girlfriend, Sharon?
No I do not.

I wouldn't want to be *his* girlfriend – that Darren. He does things under his desk in class when teacher isn't looking!

I'm going
to call for
Michael Breen.

He might buy
me a crunchy bar.

Michael Breen and Sharon Green —

we make a poem!